12/17

NEWBURYPORT PUBLIC LIBRARY

Football's All-Time Greats
RUNNING BACKS

JOSH LEVENTHAL

Black Rabbit Books

Bolt is published by Black Rabbit Books
P.O. Box 3263, Mankato, Minnesota, 56002.
www.blackrabbitbooks.com
Copyright © 2017 Black Rabbit Books

Design and Production by Michael Sellner
Photo Research by Rhonda Milbrett

All rights reserved. No part of this book may be reproduced in any form without written permission from the publisher.

Library of Congress Control Number: 2015954853

HC ISBN: 978-1-68072-043-3   PB ISBN: 978-1-68072-301-4

Printed in the United States at CG Book Printers,
North Mankato, Minnesota, 56003. PO #1796 4/16

Web addresses included in this book were working and appropriate at the time of publication. The publisher is not responsible for broken or changed links.

Image Credits

AP Images: ASSOCIATED PRESS, 9, 12, 13, 14 (middle); Bill Kostroun, 25; Brandon Wade, 6; Damian Strohmeyer, 23; Kevin Terrell, 15 (right), 21 (top); NFL, 10, 14 (left), 18, 20; Corbis: Elaine Thompson/AP/, Cover; Chris Szagola/ZUMA Press, 7 (right); George Holland/ZUMA Press, 15 (left); MSA/Icon SMI, Back Cover, 1, 26; Getty: John Iacono, 17; Reuters: Reuters Photographer, 15 (middle), 24; Shutterstock: EKS, 3, 6–7 (background), 14–15; enterlinedesign, 28–29 (field); Orgus88, 21 (bottom); Svyatoslav Aleksandrov, 31; VitaminCo, 32; USA Today: Joe Nicholson, 4–5; Matthew Emmons, 29 (top); Tim Heitman, 7 (left), 14 (right)

Every effort has been made to contact copyright holders for material reproduced in this book. Any omissions will be rectified in subsequent printings if notice is given to the publisher.

Contents

CHAPTER 1
Racing Down
the Field................4

CHAPTER 2
Running Backs from
1920 to 1965..........8

CHAPTER 3
Running Backs from
1966 to 1999.........16

CHAPTER 4
Running Backs from
2000 to Today.......22

Other Resources............30

CHAPTER 1

Racing
Down the Field

The running back stands in the backfield. The quarterback yells, "hike!" The running back runs toward him. He quickly takes the **handoff**. Then he fakes left and dodges a player. He spots a hole and races toward the goal line. *Touchdown!*

TAKING THE HANDOFF

make a pocket with both arms

Step 1

CHAPTER 2

Running Backs
from 1920 to 1965

Running backs are a key part of a team's **offense**. They run with the ball and catch passes. Running backs must be quick and strong. They also need to dodge other players.

In the early years of football, running backs' jobs were different. They still ran the ball. But sometimes they would throw it too. Running backs also played on **defense**.

Jim Thorpe

Jim Brown vs. Emmitt Smith
(1957-1965) **(1990-2004)**

3 MVP Awards **1**

9 number of times named to Pro Bowl 8

5 number of seasons led league in rushing touchdowns 3

Jim Thorpe and Jim Brown

Jim Thorpe played running back in the 1920s. He had speed and power. He could pass and catch. He could kick **field goals** from the 50-**yard** line. Thorpe is called one of the greatest athletes of all time.

Jim Brown was one of the greatest running backs ever. He led the league in **rushing** yards a record eight times. He scored more than 100 touchdowns. But he played just nine NFL seasons.

Red Grange and Bronko Nagurski

Red Grange was a running back for the Bears. He helped make pro football popular. His fast speed made him fun to watch.

Bronko Nagurski was another Bears running back. He was known to run like a bull. He pushed through anyone in his way. He gained 4,031 yards in nine seasons.

Grange was called the "Galloping Ghost."

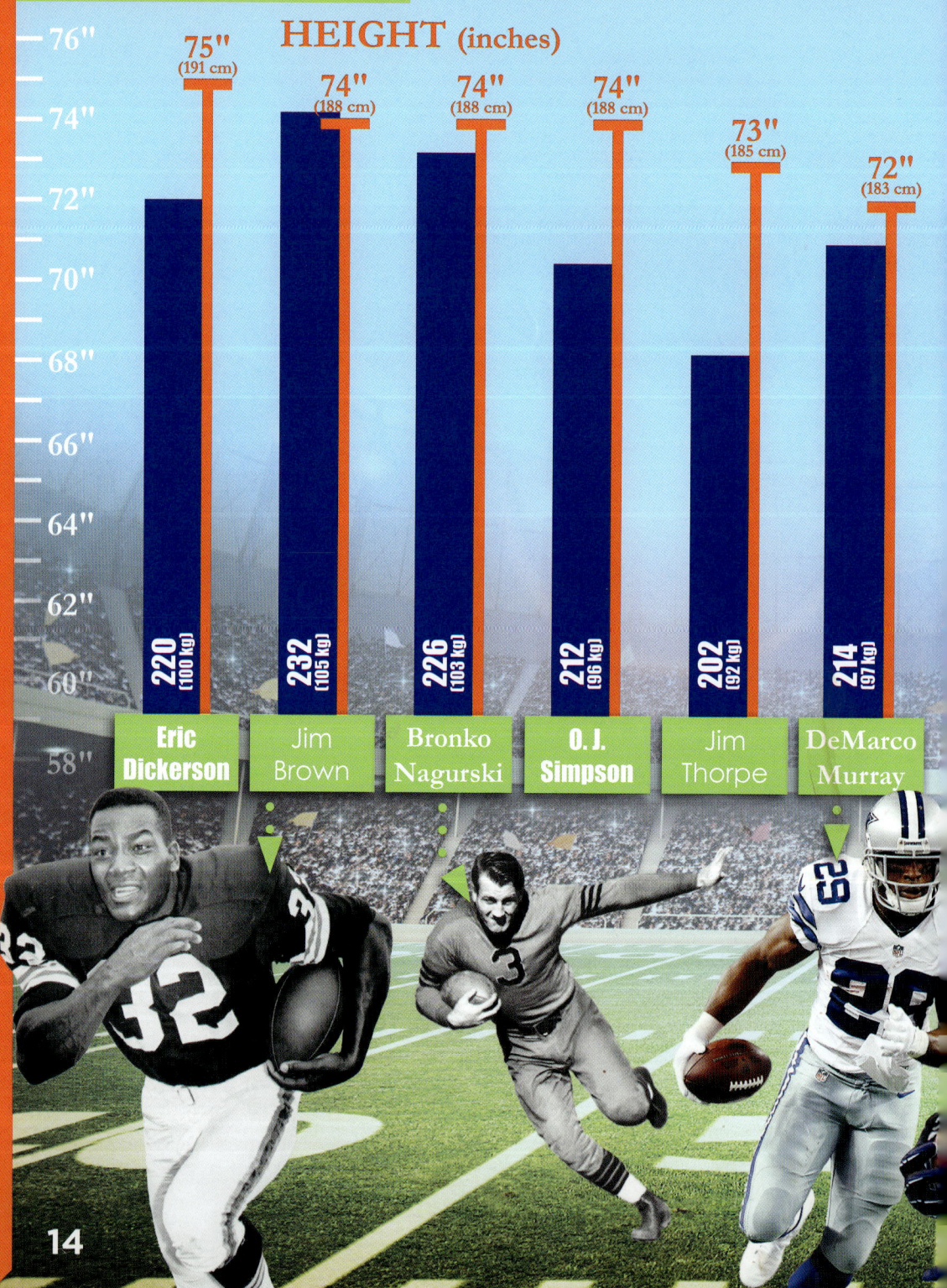

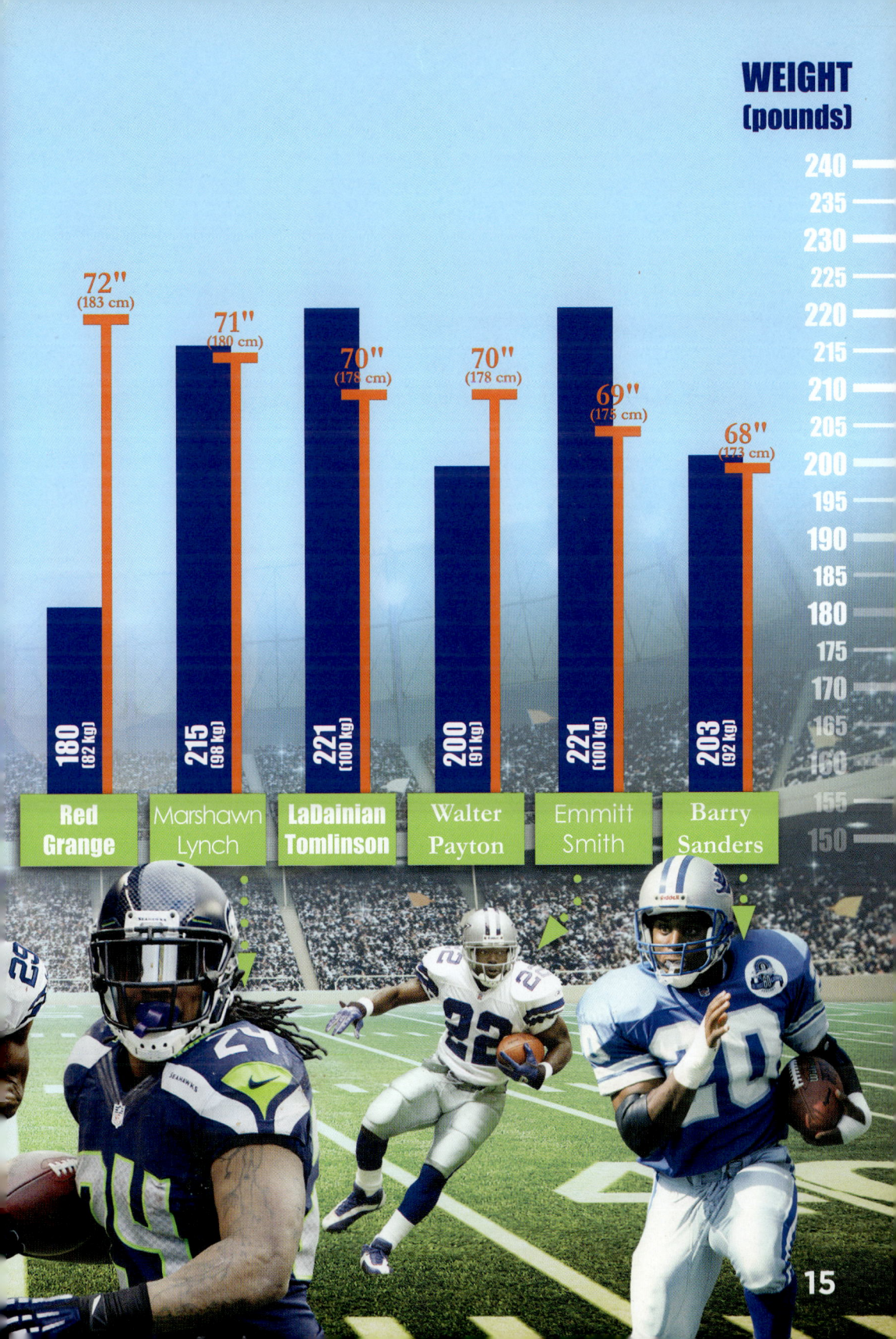

CHAPTER 3

from 1966 to 1999

In the 1970s, teams started using only one or two players to run the ball. Running backs became the stars of their teams. Many Hall of Fame running backs played during this time.

O. J. Simpson

Walter Payton

O. J. Simpson and Walter Payton

O. J. Simpson played for the Bills and 49ers. He ran for 2,003 yards in 1973. He was the first to gain 2,000 yards in one season.

Walter "Sweetness" Payton played for the Bears. He scored 125 touchdowns in his **career**. He also ran for more than 100 yards in 77 games.

Eric Dickerson

Eric Dickerson ran for 1,808 yards in his first season. It is the most ever by a **rookie**. The next year, he set an all-time record with 2,105 yards.

Barry Sanders

Barry Sanders was short, but he was quick. He ran for at least 1,000 yards every season he played. Sanders spent his whole career with the Lions.

Most Yards Run in One Season

- 2,105 — Eric Dickerson 1984
- 2,097 — Adrian Peterson 2012
- 2,066 — Jamal Lewis 2003
- 2,053 — Barry Sanders 1997
- 2,008 — Terrell Davis 1998

(through 2015 season)

CHAPTER 4

Running Backs
from 2000 to Today

Running backs today are stronger and faster than ever. Teams use fewer running plays than before. But they still need star runners.

Adrian Peterson is a running back for the Vikings. In 2007, he ran for nearly 300 yards in one game. It will be hard to break that record.

Emmitt Smith

Emmitt Smith won three Super Bowls with the Cowboys. In his career, he ran for the most yards in football history. He ran 18,355 yards. He also ran for the most touchdowns.

Most Yards in a Single Game (through 2015 season)

Adrian Peterson	Jamal Lewis
296 yards	**295 yards**

LaDainian Tomlinson

LaDainian Tomlinson was one of the best running backs of the 2000s. He had 28 rushing touchdowns in 2006. That is an all-time record.

Jerome Harrison	Corey Dillon	Walter Payton
286 yards	**278 yards**	**275 yards**

Marshawn Lynch and DeMarco Murray

Marshawn Lynch is known as "Beast Mode." He breaks tackles with his great strength. He has scored more than 70 touchdowns in his career. He also helped the Seahawks go to two Super Bowls.

DeMarco Murray led the league in running yards in 2014. He carried the ball 392 times. And he made 13 touchdowns. Fans are excited to see what he'll do in the future.

Team Runner

Watching a running back crash through the defense is exciting. A breakaway run down the field is a thrill. Teams count on these fast, strong players to score.

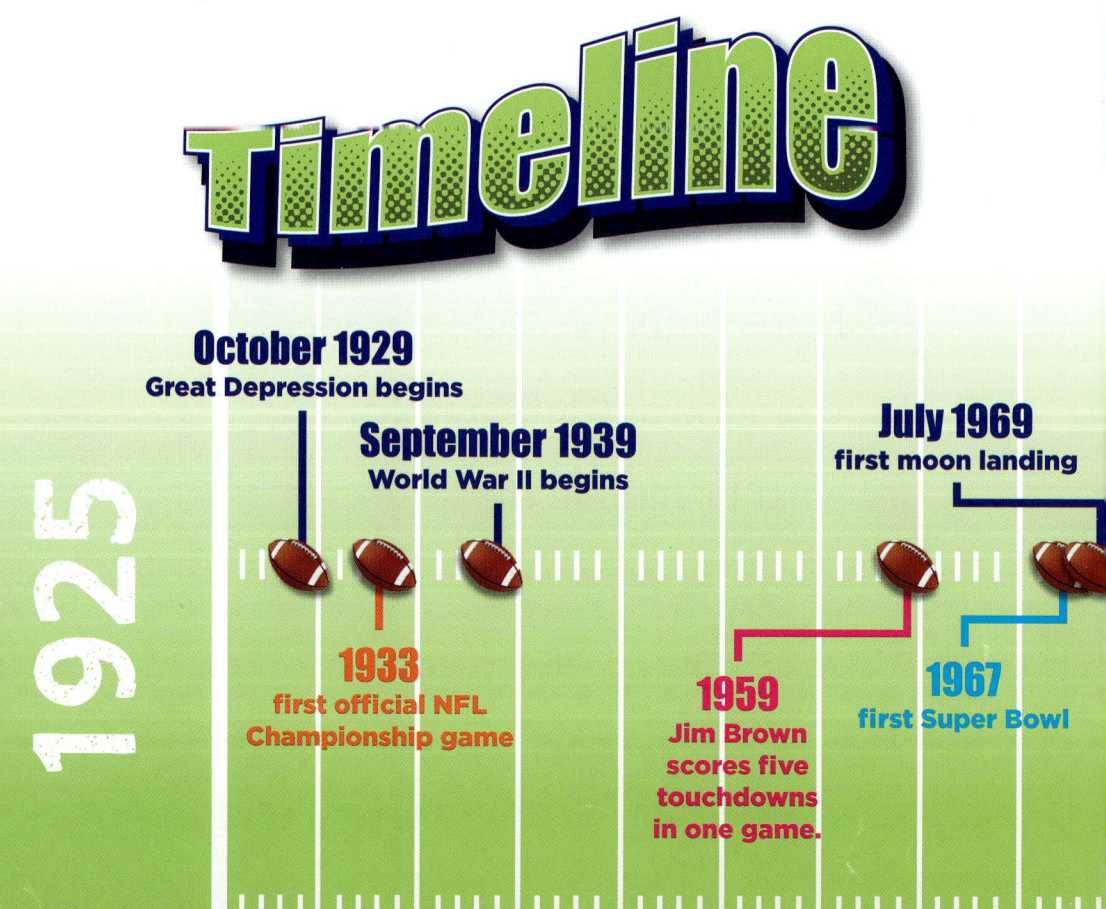

Timeline

1925

October 1929
Great Depression begins

September 1939
World War II begins

1933
first official NFL Championship game

1959
Jim Brown scores five touchdowns in one game.

July 1969
first moon landing

1967
first Super Bowl

DeMarco Murray

September 2001
terrorist attack on World Trade Center and Pentagon

1973
O. J. Simpson gains 2,000 yards in one season.

2002
Emmitt Smith breaks Walter Payton's record for career rushing yards.

2007
Adrian Peterson sets record for rushing yards in a game.

2015

GLOSSARY

career (kuh-REER)—a period of time spent in a job

defense (DEE-fens)—the players on a team who try to stop the other team from scoring

field goal (FEELD GOHL)—a score of three points made by kicking the ball between the goalposts

handoff (HAND-ohf)—the giving of a football to a teammate

offense (AW-fens)—the group of players in control of the ball trying to score points

play (PLAY)—a planned action taken in a game

rookie (ROOK-ee)—a first-year player

rushing (RUSH-ing)—moving the football toward the goal by using running plays

yard (YARD)—a unit of length; one yard equals 3 feet (1 meter).

LEARN MORE

BOOKS

Challen, Paul. *What Does a Running Back Do?* Football Smarts. New York: PowerKids Press, 2015.

Scheff, Matt. *Superstars of the Chicago Bears.* Pro Sports Superstars. Mankato, MN: Amicus High Interest, 2014.

Wilner, Barry. *Football's Top 10 Running Backs.* Top 10 Sports Stars. Berkeley Heights, NJ: Enslow Publishers, 2011.

WEBSITES

Football: Running Back
www.ducksters.com/sports/football/runningback.php

Pro Football Hall of Fame
www.profootballhof.com

INDEX

B
Brown, Jim, 10–11, 14, 28

D
Dickerson, Eric, 14, 20–21

G
Grange, Red, 12–13, 15

L
Lynch, Marshawn, 15, 27

M
Murray, DeMarco, 14, 27

N
Nagurski, Bronko, 12, 14

P
Payton, Walter, 15, 19, 25

Peterson, Adrian, 21, 22, 24, 29

S
Sanders, Barry, 15, 21

Simpson, O. J., 14, 19, 29

Smith, Emmitt, 10, 15, 24, 29

T
Thorpe, Jim, 11, 14

Tomlinson, LaDainian, 15, 25